I0717018

The Mind of a Writer

and Other Fables

Stephen Evans

This is a work of fiction. The names, characters, places, and incidents are either the products of the author's imagination or are used fictitiously, and any resemblance to actual persons living or dead, business establishments, events, or locales is entirely coincidental.

This book is dedicated to all the others who live in my head. I hope you make it out someday.

Copyright © 2024 by Stephen Evans. All rights reserved.

Second Edition- Revised

Book Layout ©2017 BookDesignTemplates.com

The Mind of a Writer and Other Fables: Stephen Evans

ISBN: 978-1953725462

"The Sound comes and goes. The music is always real."

Nick Ward

The Marriage of True Minds

Contents

Foreword

When we moved from Washington DC to Minneapolis in the early 1990s, my wife moved first. I drove up after.

My little Mercury Tracer did not have cruise control and I had two bad ankles from basketball injuries my senior year in college. So my father went with me, driving most of the way, and telling stories the whole way.

I spent three enthralled days on the road listening to him tell tales of growing up in Iowa: how he got his nickname (Trapper); every job he ever held; how he met my mother; his time in the Navy during WWII. And how he wanted to be a writer.

This was a surprise to me. I learned that after he got out of the Navy at the end of WWII, he enrolled at George Washington University to study journalism. But eventually, he had to drop out to support his young family.

Years later, after I had moved back (alone) to DC, he finally showed me a story he had kept for over half a century. It's not finished, and not anything I would have expected him to write. I don't know if there is a genetic component to writing, but his style reminds me a little of mine—quirky, fast, funny.

For most of his life, my father was a constant and intrepid reader of anything from English history to Louis L'Amour to Jean Auel's *Earth's Children* series. We shared a special passion for adventure stories from the Forties by authors like Frank Yerby and Edison Marshall, Rafeal Sabatini, and Harold Lamb. I would comb

used bookstores and bring them to him
like the lost treasures out of the tales
themselves.

Some years before my first novel *The
Marriage of True Minds* was published in
2008, he began a long slow descent into
dementia. He was not able to read my
novel, though he seemed so proud when I
showed him the published volume.
Reading was a great loss to him I know. It
had been so much of his life in his long
retirement: golf, cards, reading, and my
mother—not in that order.

Dad went into the hospital for the last
time the day after Thanksgiving in 2009.
By that time he had lost all his words. One
moment when we were alone together in
the hospital, I showed him a page in a book
I was writing called *A Transcendental
Journey*. The dedication was to him. He
made no sound, but his eyes went wide
and I truly felt he understood. It was such
a small gesture for all he had given me, but
I'm glad I was able to do it.

From time to time over his last few years, we talked about writing a book together, about his boyhood days in Iowa. He even started making notes. As I look at them now, the handwriting reflects the slow decline in his condition. I can't make out the last few words. The letters are too shaky.

I would have enjoyed writing that book. And I would have enjoyed reading it. He infused every tale with his sly humor and deep joy in the telling. I imagine he could have been quite a writer. Instead he gave me the chance to be one. I guess that's what being a father is all about.

This collection includes his story along with some pieces of mine. I hope it will stand in for that book we wanted to write together, at least until I can finish the story he started.

Heart of Gold

He was the pleasantest man I ever knew.

Well, I ever met. I didn't know him.

No one did really.

He smiled at everyone. But I never heard him say a word except to Milly, who was waitressing then down at the diner. But it wasn't his order—he didn't have to say that. He got the same thing every time, no matter what time of day he came in: Fried egg sandwich, fries, coke. All he said, all I ever heard him say anyway, was "thank you very much". I suppose at one point he must have told someone his order, because otherwise how would they know? But I never heard it.

One day while he was eating he just fell down dead. Oh, they took him to the hospital. When they got there, they cut open his chest to do surgery or something. That's when they found it.

Solid, they said. Shiny. Worth about a million dollars. Which was good, because he didn't have insurance.

Guess he didn't expect it to break.

The Island of Always

In the heart of a lake in the heart of a city in the heart of a land in the heart of the world there is an island in the shape of a heart.

The island is home to many amazing animals: a purple-and-orange giraffe who recites poetry, a red-and-blue monkey who plays the saxophone, and even a yellow-and-green snake who juggles. But none is more amazing than the Magical Dog Who Never Sleeps. The Magical Dog forever stands on guard on the shore of the island.

One fine sunny morning, a Knight in Blue Armor comes riding along through the forest and sees the island. And he thinks: "Any island in the shape of a heart with a nearsighted purple-and-orange giraffe, a red-and-blue monkey who plays the saxophone, a yellow-and-green snake who can juggle, and a Magical Dog Who Never Sleeps must be a wonderful place indeed."

So the Blue Knight calls out, "Oh, wise and wondrous Magical Dog, how may I get onto your island?"

The Magical Dog replies, because all Magical Dogs can talk, "Memory in reverse is Imagination."

"Hmmm," says the Blue Knight. "Should I swim to the island? Should I jump? Should I pole-vault?"

But the Magical Dog only says again: "Memory in reverse is Imagination."

"Ahhh," thinks the Blue Knight. Then he kneels down by the water's edge and, seeing his reflection in the calm, shiny surface, dips his right hand through the image, lifts the water up in his palm, then casts the glittering droplets up into the air. Suddenly a rainbow stretches from the shore of the lake all the way onto the island. Then the Blue Knight stands and walks over the rainbow bridge onto the enchanted island.

And the Blue Knight abides on the island in the shape of a heart while the purple-and-orange giraffe recites poetry, while the red-and-blue monkey plays marching songs, while the yellow-and-green snake juggles two pomegranates, a teacup, and the knight's very sharp sword. Finally the Blue Knight thinks that it must be time to leave, so he says: "Oh wise and wondrous Magical Dog, this is a very fine island, but how does one get off?"

"Beats me," the Magical Dog replies. "Why do you think I'm still here?"

"No. Seriously," says the Blue Knight.

So the Magical Dog laughs and says: "Imagination in reverse is Memory."

And so the Blue Knight kneels down once more at the water's edge and dips his left hand into his image and again casts the glistening droplets into the air. Once more a rainbow appears, and the Blue Knight crosses back over the many-colored bridge onto the lakeshore.

But when the Blue Knight turns to say good-bye, he sees himself still standing on the island. So he asks the Magical Dog: "Oh, wise and wondrous Magical Dog, why do I see myself still standing on the island next to you?"

And the Magical Dog replies: "On this island, there is no time. No day. No night. No past. No future. There isn't even any Now. There is only Always. If you are ever here, you are always here."

And the Blue Knight replies: "Then I won't say good-bye," and he turns and walks away.

A Visitor to your Planet

At Rise: A man is doing something.

(An alien enters and watches him.)

ALIEN
Why are you doing that?

MAN
Needs doing.

ALIEN
How do you know?

MAN
It's my work.

ALIEN
What is work?

MAN
What needs doing.

ALIEN

I'm asking you.

MAN

I'm telling you.

ALIEN

What is my work?

MAN

Asking questions.

ALIEN

That is my work!

MAN

You're good at your job.

(Long pause)

ALIEN

I am a visitor to your planet.

(Long pause)

MAN

Aren't we all?

BLACKOUT

Mulberry Pie

I hear tell Reverend Larson used to climb up inside the steeple and shine that bell twice a year, shine it so you could see it a mile or more. But no one had touched it in years.

The church was way back at the end of Trumpeter road, up against a hill. There was a white mulberry tree, an old one, maybe fifty feet tall and near as wide, just at the top where the hill curled around the church. If you stood outside the church door just so, it looked like the steeple ended in mulberries. I'd ride out that way on my bike after school when the berries were ripe and I wasn't needed at the store.

I climbed up past the blackened patch then up over the split twist in the trunk to my spot, about twenty feet up, where no other I fancied had ever rested and I was invisible to the world. I plucked a few berries and leaned back to enjoy, until the breeze picked up and mulberries began to rain around me.

Sister Larson, Mrs. Larson, the Reverend's wife, still lived in the house next the church. Out she came and lifted her apron to shade the sun away, gazing up.

"Well glory," she said, "Alma Jean, get down out that tree. And bring me some of those mulberries," and went inside.

Not so invisible, I slid back down to earth now covered in white fruit. Mrs. Larson's mulberry pie was legend in Webster County, though it had not been seen at the Fair for years, not since the Reverend passed, before I was born. But I had heard sighs in the telling. So I lifted my shirt to make a basket, gathered handfuls of the fallen berries among those

I had not scrunched underfoot, and hurried after her.

I edged the porch door open with my elbow to keep from losing any of the berries to the floor. Once inside, I dumped them into Sister's apron. She carried them to the washbasin and poured them into a glass bowl on the counter beside.

"White mulberries are the key. This is the only white mulberry tree in the county. My husband planted it for me the year we moved in. Took ten years before we saw the first fruit. And the next year I won the prize. That was in, well, long ago."

She turned back toward me.

"Oh Lord," she said.

I looked behind me but no one was there and when I turned back Sister Larson was reaching for my shirt.

"Can't send you back to your mother in a shirt looking like that," she said. "Wrap yourself in that tablecloth, and give me that shirt."

"But," I said, and held out hands, which were covered with berry juice.

"Yes, you're right. That wouldn't do to get berry stains all over my good linen. And if there's one thing I have learned in life it is how to get out a mulberry stain. I fought mulberry stains like my husband fought the devil, you might say. But I reckon I won more often than he did, bless his tired soul."

She pulled me over to the sink and scrubbed my hands with vinegar then lemon. "That tablecloth," she said, "was given to me as a wedding present from Henry's, the Reverends, grandmother, who had it from her grandmother, so she said. There. That should do it. "

And it did. Not a sign left of stain.

"Now dry your hands on that towel. And give me that shirt, young lady."

The cloth was laid neatly over the back of the chair. It felt solid, smooth from so many a Thanksgiving or Easter feast. I turned my back, slipped off my shirt, and wrapped myself in the cloth white as clouds soft as snow and still warm from the iron.

Mrs. Larson laid her hands on her hips and laughed.

"Well, if there had been a female apostle, you could be her double."

I looked in the mirror next the back door and had to smile on myself. The tablecloth covered everything from my overalls down to almost my sneakers. I did look sort of holy. I could have shucked my shoes and snuck right into the Christmas pageant and no one would have mussed a hair. It was also as close as I had ever come to wearing a dress. That I could remember. Can't say for when I was little. But even in pictures I always dressed like a boy. I pulled the cloth tighter around me, and felt the warmth slide up the back of my knees, which gave me shivers.

I sat on the kitchen chair nearest the window and peeked out behind the curtain. I couldn't quite see the church, so anyone at the church couldn't have quite seen me. I looked west, over the town, across the valley. Shadows of clouds flowed fast across the new plowed fields with the alfalfa still underground.

"Come away from that window, Alma Jean," Sister commanded. "Come sit over here and I will teach you something about pies."

I wrapped the tablecloth tight around me and stood. It was hard to walk. I had to kind of shuffle one foot in front of the other. I imagined this was what it was like to walk in those long dresses I had seen in the movies.

I pulled up a stool next to Sister and sat. The berries were in a white bowl, juices already pooling at the bottom. She picked each berry, eyed it all around like a jewel, swished it gently in a second white bowl, eyed it again, then placed it in a third bowl or tossed it in a tin can in the sink. She was humming something I thought I knew but couldn't name. A hymn, I guess. The other church down the road they sing lots of new songs. This sounded old, not so much up and down jumping but smooth and a little hop now and then. I liked it.

"With a tree like this you don't really need to wash the berries. Fruit from the market you should wash always but this no. I do it anyway. Sometimes when you are washing you'll see something in a berry that you didn't notice before, how it doesn't quite fit with the others colorwise or size. You don't need them all the same but consistency in the berry smooths out the filling once it's baked to where it's almost like a cream pie. That's one secret I can share."

Thunder rumbled outside. Sister glanced toward the window.

"Bring me that kindling."

She shuffled over to an old black woodstove in the corner. I grabbed an armload of tree limb chopped small and even, balancing it away from the tablecloth which I held in a tightfisted twist to my chest.

"Most things I cook in the oven now," she said, stoking the stove with kindling. I had never seen a stove like that except in movies. "But you can't bake a fruit pie in an electric oven. The heat is too dry. You need wood fire for a real pie."

She walked to an old hutch next to the pantry door, reached high up to the top shelf, and pulled down three rolling pins. The largest was big around as my fist, the next two fingers wide, and the third narrow as a thumb.

"If you want a light crust, you can't do with just one rolling pin. You need at least three to flow down, heavy to medium to light."

She took the dough out the refrigerator, sprinkled it with flour, and began rolling with the heavy pin: half a roll, sprinkle, back; half a roll, sprinkle, back, all the way across. Then she gently raised and turned the dough a quarter around and began with the medium pin: half a roll, sprinkle, back; half a roll, sprinkle, back, many more times than the first.

"A heavy pin will tear a light crust. These I had the Reverend make out of a branch off that Mulberry tree, sheared off by lightening, thirty year ago now. The Reverend was good with his hands. He did his own work on the church back then, loved to take off the frock coat and put on his overalls. Don't like the thought of it falling to anyone else now. He took such pride in it."

Thunder again. Closer. And wind. I edged my way toward the window to see.

"Away from there, girl. Want someone to see you dressed the way you are?" Sister warned.

I ducked quick. A ridiculous sight I must have looked in that getup. Still I listened out when Sister was not talking, which wasn't often. I guess she had little company out here these days and took advantage.

"Come over here, Alma, and watch this. This no one else will ever teach you."

I shuffled back to her side and slid onto the stool, careful for splinters. I wound my legs around the legs of the stool to keep from swinging them, which I have a habit of. But I couldn't help tapping my feet against the brace. Some things you can't help.

Sister took a lemon and sliced it in two.

"The white mulberry is the sweetest of the fruits. And some will tell you to add lemon to the filling to give it tartness. And that's fine. But my secret is, which no one knows but me, and now you, you don't put the lemon in the filling: you sprinkle the juice of two lemons over the crust before baking. Then the filling and the crust stay pure in themselves, but when eaten together the pure sweet and pure tart revolve in the mouth, changing a mite with every piece and every bite and even every chew. I have never told this to another soul, Alma Jean, and you must swear to pass it on only to your children."

I said "I swear, Sister" but I wasn't thinking of pie right then because it had never occurred to me before that I might have children. Right then I didn't think it was likely but later I thought well if ever then it would be worthy to have secrets to pass on to only her or him or them as the case.

Sister opened a drawer and took hold of a wide blade knife. She scooped and spread the mulberry filling across the crust like she was bricking a wall. Then she finished over with a lattice cover until the pie looked like a round checkerboard.

Sister held the pie up over her head like she was offering it to the Lord. Then in a motion I couldn't quite fix she pulled and lifted and kicked the stove door with her foot, the pie somehow inside.

"How long?" I asked.

Then the church bell rang.

If Sister had not had the pie in the oven already I swear she would have dropped it, so surprised she was to hear that bell. And me right with her. That bell had not rung in all my life.

The bell rang again.

And again.

I ran out the door, tablecloth and all. It was storm dark overhead though light east and west, and the wind was high, so the cloth spread out behind me like a cape. I barely held onto it and felt bad when the rain started to drop that Sister's cherished linen might be ruined. But I wasn't about to let go.

The bell rang about eight or nine more times. The wind I guess. No one up there that I could see. All up and down Trumpeter people came out to see and stood there in the deep rain to listen to that bell.

Some say the last knell sounded before the lightning. Some say after. To me, they happened the same. I blinked at the deafening crack and opened to the old Mulberry tree smoking and split open to the ground.

The rain stopped and the wind and we stopped too and stared at the smoldering. Then a wave of sweetness took us over and we nearly all swooned to the ground with the aroma, as if we could taste the air around us, sweet and heady, not a breath of tartness, as if the rain had been not water but honey, the hail not ice but sugar, as if God's sharp knife had cut into the biggest juiciest pie ever baked.

This was what heaven must smell like, I thought, not lavender or frankincense or myrrh, but home-baked woodfired mulberry pie. We knelt on the wet lawn of the church, inhaled the glory, and were glad.

Down with Moonlight

At Rise: Kay and Zed are sitting in the moonlight.

KAY

I love you madly.

(Long pause)

ZED

Is there another way?

KAY

You don't understand.

ZED

You.

KAY

What?

ZED

You.

                    Kay

What?

                    Zed

I don't understand you. I understand a lot
of things. Just not you.

                    Kay

Like what?

                    Zed

Double entry accounting.

                    Kay

Ah.

                    Zed

Quantum mechanics.

                    Kay

Oh.

                    Zed

The mind of God.

                    Kay

But not me.

                    Zed

No.

KAY

Why?

ZED

You love me madly.

KAY

Is there another way?

ZED

Exactly.

KAY

No. I'm asking.

ZED

It's a good question.

(PAUSE)

KAY

Down with moonlight.

(LONG PAUSE)

ZED

Where else would it go?

BLACKOUT

Anne Hathaway Remembers

They say that he was good, but I don't know. I never left this town in all my life. It was he one day came back to me. What he left behind I cannot say. He could talk. Oh Lord, could he be sweet. No sweeter man drew breath, that I am sure. Young he was, and quiet, when we met. Handfasted in the spring of '82, wed by winter, child inside, Susanna, next the twins, then after, he was gone. And so it was, twenty years with letters, only words, words and words to live on, words to dream on, and I did, each night hid safe beneath me in our second-best bed.

STEPHEN EVANS

The Peddler Who Sold Nothing

Once upon a time there was a peddler who sold nothing. He drove from town to town with an empty wagon pulled by an old black and white horse named Erwin. No one ever knew the peddler's name, because no one ever asked.

"Well, peddler," they would say when he came to town, "what have you to sell today?"

"Nothing," he would reply, and they would all laugh.

"Why should we buy nothing from you?" they would say. "We have enough of that already!"

The peddler would only smile and laugh along with them, and move along to the next town.

Year after year, town to town, he rode, always offering to sell nothing. Always they declined, and always he laughed. But each year his laugh grew louder and louder and his clothes grew finer and finer and his cart grew grander and grander.

Someone must be buying his nothing, the people thought, though no one could figure out why. But perhaps there was something to this nothing after all. Each one looked at his neighbor and wondered if it were he who was buying nothing. Perhaps they were hoarding nothing, and someday when the village needed nothing, there would not be enough to go around. For they realized that they really knew nothing about nothing.

Finally, one brave soul came to the peddler secretly and asked to buy nothing. "Nothing is very expensive," the peddler said, holding out a document and pen "and for it you must give everything".

"I must have nothing," the man cried, signing the document. He went and got all his money and all his worldly goods and piled them in front of the peddler. Then the peddler reached into his cart, pulled out a sword, and cut off the man's head.

"Now," said the peddler, "no one will ever have more nothing than you."

Then he took the man's money and goods, loaded them into his cart, and drove away.

Erwin whinnied once.

"Yes," said the peddler, "Nothing is so tempting as nothing."

Erwin whinnied twice.

"It is not a tautology, it's folk wisdom," replied the peddler. "Now if I said Nothing is as tempting as nothing, that would be a tautology."

Erwin whinnied three times.

The peddler shook his head and said "No, it is not a semantic distinction, it is a logical one."

Erwin snorted.

"Look," began the peddler, "in the Tractatus Logico-Philosophicus, Wittgenstein defined a tautology as..." and the discussion continued the whole way home to the palace.

The Circus of the Animal Crackers

It bothers me that my animal crackers don't all face the same direction.

Also I can't tell the rhinos from the hippos.

Which is important because hippos are more dangerous in milk.

My mother says eating animal crackers involves a complicated ethos.

She says Ethos is Greek for Because I Said So.

I think it may also be the name of one of the three musketeers.

I saw that movie with my father.

They had swords and mustaches.

I liked the swords.

I keep giving them names.

I'm almost ready to eat one and then I think Dave.

Or Ron.

Or Ethos.

Dave is my favorite.

I'm definitely eating him last.

Or George.

George has a broken head.

He may go first.

Or maybe I will free them all.

And we'll start a circus.

The Circus of the Animal Crackers.

I'll be the Ringmaster.

But I won't have a mustache.

I'll have a sword.

STEPHEN EVANS

Well, There's this Pond

Scene: A publisher's office.

At Rise: Henry David Thoreau,
               manuscript in hand, is sitting
               across from the publisher.

PUBLISHER
I read your book. What is it called?
Waldo?

THOREAU
Walden, or Life in the Woods.

PUBLISHER
So you went to the woods.

THOREAU
Precisely.

PUBLISHER
And?

THOREAU

What do you mean?

PUBLISHER

What happened?

THOREAU

I built a cabin.

PUBLISHER

And?

THOREAU

I grew beans.

PUBLISHER

Was there a giant beanstalk or something?

THOREAU

No, just regular beans.

PUBLISHER

Maybe someone attacked you in the woods.

THOREAU

No. I had a few guests.

PUBLISHER

Were you molested as a child? Is that why you went to the woods.

THOREAU
I went to the woods to live deliberately.

PUBLISHER
Or were you an alcoholic maybe? We could call it A Drunk in the Woods.

THOREAU
I don't drink.

PUBLISHER
Did you catch some disfiguring disease? Maybe from the beans?

THOREAU
Sorry.

PUBLISHER
I don't get it. Why would anyone buy this book? Explain it to me again.

THOREAU
Well, there's this pond...

BLACKOUT

STEPHEN EVANS

Mrs. Evans Remembers

He wasn't exactly fun. Not exactly. He would have wanted me to be exact. Or precise. Or maybe clear. At first I thought that he was funny. He made me laugh. And he could write. He didn't, but he could, and that intrigued me. What else? What else? Oh. And sometimes, he would talk, sometimes, for hours, late at night. And he would hold me like the breeze, all over but not tight enough to frighten. He wasn't sweet exactly—there's that word—but he was thoughtful. Or, at least, he thought. Sometimes warm. Often not there at all. I always wondered where he went, sitting in my leather chair, and how, as I was watching him the whole blessed time.

STEPHEN EVANS

The Mind of a Writer

My left shoe is untied.

It has become untied before.

Perhaps this is because I am right-handed and it is harder to tie my left shoe.

Possibly this is a symptom of a serious neurological condition known as Left-Shoe-Tying Disorder.

I have LSTD.

I wonder if there is an LSTD support group.

I should tie my left shoe before I trip.

I will tie my left shoe.

I wonder how long it will be before it comes untied again.

I should write down the time so I can see how long it takes.

I should create a spreadsheet to track Left Shoe Untying Events.

I have LSUE.

I should write an algorithm to determine the mean time between LSUEs.

Ouch.

I wonder if I tripped because my left shoe was untied.

I should write a story about that.

Then I should tie my left shoe.

Frosty versus the Zombie Apocalypse

Heedless of the approaching holiday celebration, or anything else, the zombies lurched across the snow-covered town square toward the cowering children. Frosty was their only hope.

Quickly, the wily snow man organized his young charges, gathering their hats, and urging them to build an army of snow men. The children, who had much experience, worked quickly, ever mindful of the advancing mindless horde. As each was finished and Frosty crowned it with a child's hat, it magically sprang to life, determined to protect its young creator at all costs.

When all the hats were situated, Frosty examined his army. The clever children had sculpted not just snow men, but snow lions, snow tigers, snow bears, snow dragons, and even snow dinosaurs. Frosty turned toward the zombies with coal eyes afire, lifted his corncob pipe high in the air, and gave the order to charge.

No one knows what happened to either the snow army or the zombies. Both were enveloped in a blizzard of white as the two deadly forces met. When the battle was done and the children safe, all that was left was a pile of hats and two lumps of coal. The corncob pipe was never recovered.

So the children of Whistletown believe that he is still out there somewhere, probably somewhere refrigerated, waiting until he is needed once again. On Christmas morning now, all the children leave their hats on their snowy front lawns, in remembrance of the bravery and sacrifice of one magical snowman known simply as Frosty.

The Dance

Truth does not require words, so words conspire against it.

Whatever else I say, remember this: I went into a dirty tavern and danced with drunken old men. That is the human truth of it. There may be other truths, but what good are they to us?

A true son of my generation, I was wandering through Europe to find myself. My hair was not too long, nor my beard remarkable. My chief claim to notoriety was my leather Apache boots, hand made by an old Navajo Indian. Why a Navajo was making Apache boots is even now beyond my historical expertise. He was a shaman and the boots fit, so I really didn't care.

My traveling companions had taken it upon themselves to improve my asceticism by leaving in the middle of the night with my car and most of my other possessions. I am not being cynical here; they truly believed this. I have seen each of them since and they expected to be thanked for the favor. I am not going to tell you what I said.

They left my guitar and my money. I am rich, by the way. At the time I was carrying a considerable amount of money, which I suppose lends credence to my friends' story. We had been sleeping on a beach a short distance from a little town in Eastern Europe, I don't know which country, but for semantic and sentimental reasons I would guess it was Greece. The village was one of fishermen, the type who eat what they catch. To live, for those of you unaware of this quaint custom.

I woke up wet and cold. I assume it had rained while I was sleeping, though I am not sure.

I walked into town and entered the only lighted building I could see. Men were there, drinking. Another night, they would have I can imagine them gladly taking me out back and breaking both my arms. Only then would they have killed me and taken my money. I must have come on a holiday or something. Anyway I was in no mood to care whether they wanted to kill me or not. I am something of a killer myself, though in a less casual way. At any rate, I walked to what looked like a bar, placed a bill on the counter and pointed to a bottle. The barkeep stared at me, then at the bill, then shrugged and gave it to me. I got no change.

I took the bottle and walked over to a table, sat leaning against the wall taking long drinks of whatever it was in the bottle. Most of the men did not move. Some glared. One came over to the table, took my bottle, and took a long drink from it. When he put it down, I stood up, picked up the bottle and broke it over his head. He fell and did not move. I got myself another bottle and returned to my seat against the wall. The other men in the room got up and walked over to the one lying on the floor. They looked at him, then at me. Then they picked up their fallen comrade and carried him out the door. I gathered later that no one really liked him anyway.

The oldest one of the lot sat down next to me and offered me a drink from a dirty wineskin he kept around his neck. The wine was mixed with something else a little more potent, maybe hashish. Soon, the whole crowd was gathered at my table, trading drinks and my cigarettes. They told me their funny stories and I roared with laughter. I told them mine and they roared back. We didn't understand each other.

From somewhere they produced a wretched little mandolin and the music was accompanied by hands clapping and feet pounding. I took out my guitar and tried to play along. I don't know if I succeeded.

Three of the old men started dancing in slow rhythm. The clapping became more uniform and the pounding stopped. The mandolin insinuated a melody very much different from the one it had begun, the song older, the harmonics odd.

The three men moved as one line, stooping, twisting, and even drinking in absolute unison. They made me join the line, against my wishes. I had no desire to disturb the ancient motion of their dance.

The eyes of the men were blind, and my eyes nearly so. They stared ahead unfocused, or focused on something beyond my perception. They stared anyway. The music became the single entity, enveloping, rolling all the men and wine and mind. Blankness shifting in and out the music changed again. Perhaps the last free thought I had was that the melody no was longer triadic but rather perfect fifths. I found I had no trouble following the rhythm of the men at first and matched them step for step, guided by the foul breath on either side of me. The mandolin no longer attempted melody. The music twitched and flowed unevenly as a river in flood and still the old men kept in step and still I stayed with them no longer even listening to the music but maybe to what the music listened to, an ebb and flow which no sea had ever followed and rising out of the dance a pattern which I saw but could not understand because I was inside it and it took me with it and.

I knew I would get carried away.

The next morning when I awoke all the old men were gone. I walked out of the tavern and the town was deserted save for one old man whom I recognized but who did not seem to know me. I walked out of that village and never went back.

I still say that I went into a dirty tavern and danced with the old men.

I say it often.

Infinity to One

Doctor Winthrop Rogers walked down the hall, disgusted. The scene he had just witnessed in the so-called conference room filled him with professional outrage.

"Circus room is what they should call it," he growled as he charged down towards his office (Doctor Rogers was a very large, very determined man). Yet there was a lightness in his step which belied his angry mood. Deep down, he was as excited as he had ever been, and not even a room full of reporters could dull the feeling for long.

Dr. Sherman Ainsley, head of the international consortium that sponsored the program, ran up from behind Rogers and attempted to corral him.

"Ah, Doctor Rogers, I am so glad I found you."

Ainsley wisely stepped to the side as Rogers barreled past him, but did not desist, sidestepping up the corridor to keep pace.

"Our guests were somewhat upset when you departed the conference so suddenly," Ainsley continued. "I do hope you'll come back. There were some very important people present. Important to you as well as to the University. After all this is your project."

Rogers stopped and glared.

"Ainsley, I haven't the slightest intention of rejoining that madhouse. I have never been so thoroughly humiliated in my life."

He started and stopped so quickly that Ainsley almost ran into him.

"Excuse me, Doctor Rogers, could you explain simply the essence of your theory in two-syllable words or less? Yes, Doctor Rogers, but it hardly took a genius to figure that out. Excuse me, Doctor, but isn't this whole project an attempt by the government to get the minds of the people off the unemployment rate? You spent HOW much for this project? And on and on."

Rogers started and stopped again, and this time Ainsley did bump into him, though he hardly noticed.

"And you didn't help much, you know," Rogers said. "I could have sworn you were enjoying it."

Ainsley had known Rogers for years. Rogers had stayed in pure research, while Ainsley had diverted to Administration, which Rogers had never let him forget. Rogers was a scientist; Ainsley was merely a bureaucrat. So it was possible, Ainsley thought, that he had enjoyed Rogers' humiliation the tiniest bit. But neither of them would enjoy the projects funding being yanked, which is what might happen if Rogers did not play nice with the press.

"Come now, Rogers," Ainsley cajoled. "It wasn't as bad as all that. Of course they were asking questions; that's their job. And they were only asking the questions their readers will ask when they read about this, and therefore it is crucial that the proper answers be given. That is why I asked you to be there in the first place. When I have to face the Grant Committee next month, we had better have some favorable constituent reaction or this project is dead. And the reporters in that room are just the ones to get it for you."

During his speech, Ainsley had somehow managed to turn Rogers around and start walking back down the corridor.

"Besides," Ainsley continued, "no matter how they seem on the outside, they are just normal people who want to believe in this project of yours. They know that if it works, they will have witnessed a landmark of human civilization. Play on that, Rogers. You believe in this thing. Let them see that. Pretty soon the whole room will be on your side. I know it."

Rogers sighed, nodded.

"Alright, if I have to, I have to. But I feel ridiculous pandering to people who don't know a gravity field from a football field."

Ainsley patted Rogers on the back, while giving him the tiniest shove back towards the conference room.

"It will all be over before you know it, and then you'll be the most famous scientist this side of Einstein."

They continued down the corridor in silence for a moment.

"Just between you and me," Ainsley added, "it will work, won't it? With the buildup I've given this thing, it better, or we won't be able to get unemployment benefits, much less continued funding."

Rogers stopped and confronted Ainsley. He spoke slowly.

"I'll say it again. We do not know what the results will be until the program has completed processing the data. You have to understand that one of the fastest supercomputers in the world has been working continuously on this for sixteen months."

He started again without waiting for Ainsley, who again sidestepped his way down the corridor. It was easier this time, since Rogers was not in a hurry.

"I understand that. I wanted this to be the real thing, not simply a demonstration of a discovery made alone in some lab. It will be much more dramatic, this way. Our television ratings will go sky high."

"Television? What do you mean television?"

"Didn't I tell you? We'll be on worldwide television, via satellite. Nearly a billion people are expected to watch. Almost as many as the Oscars."

Rogers steeled his mind to the ordeal.

"This can't be happening," he muttered and walked back into the conference room. As soon as he stepped behind the podium, a reporter held up his hand and asked.

"'Doctor Rogers, could you give us your definition of genius?"

"Certainly. A genius is someone who has the good luck not to see beyond the obvious."

Polite laughter echoed its way around the room. Another reporter chimed in.

"Thank you, Doctor. Now tell us, do you think you qualify as a genius?"

"I consider my presence before this gathering sufficient proof of the contrary."

A short, bearded man stepped forward.

"Doctor Rogers, do you really think that your device will indicate without question whether or not there are intelligent life forms in outer space?"

"The answer to that is no. The odds that there are other intelligent species like ours somewhere in the universe are so high that they might almost be called infinity to one: pure certainty. However, our experiment will determine whether the likely conditions for intelligent life exist locally, which is to say, within our galaxy."

"So, is that a yes or no?"

Rogers found resources of patience he didn't know he had. His teaching background began to reassert itself, and he almost imagined himself addressing graduate students once again.

"Let me explain again. In the data from the Voyager space probes, we discovered an anomalous signal emanating from inside our planetary system. Over the years, we have been able to determine that the source of that signal is the Earth itself. Experiments since confirmed that any rotating biomass greater than say one half the size of our planet will produce a unique electromagnetic signature. This signature is very weak and generally it gets lost in the ambient radiation of the galaxy. Beyond our galaxy, it is not likely detectable in the foreseeable future. However, thanks to our international consortium, and the generous funding of various institutions and the US Government, we finally have the computer processing power to isolate that signature within our own galaxy. The program has been running continuously now for nearly sixteen months evaluating intergalactic radiation sources, and we expect final results here today."

"So basically," added the bearded man, "you are doing what amounts to a billion-dollar virus scan of the galaxy."

Ainsley stepped in and hijacked the microphone.

"Thank you, Doctor Rogers, for that wonderful explanation. Now, if you will all accompany me to the auditorium, we can see scientific history being made."

Rogers lagged behind the rest as they paraded down the corridor to the auditorium, bubbling in their enthusiasm. Something lingered in the back of his mind, something that refused to be pulled into consciousness.

Ainsley stepped forward.

"Therefore, honored dignitaries, guests, ladies and gentlemen of the media, peoples of the world. We are now ready to commence what may well be the most spectacular broadcast in human history. Doctor Rogers, if you please!"

Rogers looked over at his co-investigator, Dr. Jennifer Wilson, and nodded his head. Wilson turned on the projector.

The screen showed one text field: Source Signatures Evaluated, and a number that flashed far too fast to be identified, but appeared to be in the range of twenty digits.

Nothing else happened for seven hours. Rogers explained that they did not know exactly when the computer would complete its processing. However, he was confident in his expectation that the processing would be completed that day.

It wasn't.

Nor was it completed the next day.

As each day passed, a feeling grew inside Dr. Rogers. The first day, he wasn't sure what it was. Nor the second. By the third day, he had identified the feeling: it was fear. But he did not know what he was afraid of. By the fifth day, he dismissed the feeling. He was good at that.

Six days, 21 hours, and seven minutes later, there were only four people in the room: Rogers, Dr. Wilson, Dr. Ainsley, the bearded man, and a lone TV cameraman. Only Dr. Wilson was awake when the number stopped flashing at 31,415,926,535,897,932.

Under the number, the words 'Processing Complete' appeared.

Dr. Wilson woke the others, then pushed a few keys. The label 'Source Signatures Identified' appeared, followed by a number: 0.

They stared for a moment.

Rogers moved to one corner of the room and sat on a stool looking thoughtful, yet not shocked.

Ainsley charged towards Rogers, followed by the bearded man. Dr. Wilson began typing furiously at the keyboard.

"How could you do it?" Ainsley bellowed. "This program will be a laughingstock, a cautionary tale. You and I are ruined and probably will be indicted.

How could it happen? How could it not work?"

Rogers looked up, puzzled. He looked over at Dr. Wilson, who nodded. He turned back to Dr. Ainsley.

"What are you talking about?"

Ainsley seemed about to explode.

"What do you mean, what am I talking about? I'm talking about your multi-million dollar bamboozle, that's what I'm talking about. That idiot program of yours which couldn't find an alien if it walked up and introduced itself, and obviously hasn't had anything to do with intelligent life from the very beginning."

Rogers stared back, seemingly unconcerned.

"It's the one thing we hadn't expected. I mean, the odds against it ..." He trailed off.

Ainsley was the one who looked perplexed, and then concerned.

"It's okay, Rogers. I understand. The shock, everything. You'll be alright. Don't worry. It's probably just a malfunction, coding error or something."

Rogers laughed.

"You don't understand."

"What?"

Rogers looked over at Dr. Wilson, who nodded. He turned back to Dr. Ainsley.

"The infinity to one shot came through."

An eerie silence settled over the room.

Rogers laughed again.

"The program worked perfectly. Exactly as it was supposed to. Only there was nothing to find."

"What do you mean?"

"I mean," Rogers said to the TV camera.

"We're alone."

STEPHEN EVANS

Mrs. Emerson Remembers

I was not his first love. That was her. Beautiful and dead at twenty. What Mature woman could compete with that? We named our eldest daughter after her. Ellen. He asked. I agreed. You see I knew. Ellen would be my child and not his wife in time. Though I did not then comprehend how long In Time could be when one is married. Now I know. Now I have learned In Time. My name he changed. From Lydia to Lidian. He needed something grander I suppose. Jackson or Emerson, I knew who I was. My Asia as well. And Mrs. Emerson When he was cross. A sweet man, all in all, even sweeter as he faded late. Our Waldo, we lost. Broke his heart, and mine. After

Waldo nothing was the same. Dear Henry too. Nothing more to say. And the house. My old house, burned away. We sent him off. I was the one to stay and try to put our seasons back in place. He went to Egypt. Edith came to me. If that was not our life, then I don't know. He mourned his books. I mourned, what did I mourn? A cushion I had mended just that day. A hat that I had always meant to wear. A pie left cooling on the windowsill. Did I mourn there was no more to mourn? No. My accumulations were not singed. She had two years. I had forty-seven. She the preacher, I the famous sage. She the passion, I the children. She the life and I the living. She was his first and maybe only love. But it was my quince apple pie he asked for at the last.

Lake of the Isles

In the early 1800s, the chief lumberjack of the northern woods was the legendary giant and frontiersman Paul Bunyan. But one day in the summer of 1836, Paul lifted his head and looked far out over the Minnesota territory and the great forest that he loved. Everywhere he saw the desolation that he and his fellow lumbermen had wreaked. And he realized that the ruin he had caused could never be undone. Devastated by this vision, Paul grew despondent and great tears began to fall from his gigantic eyes.

For weeks that summer, Paul traveled all over the Minnesota territory, from logging camp to logging camp, from grove to ancient grove, begging forgiveness from the trees he had wronged. But the voices of the trees had been stilled forever by the axes and saws and spikes of the lumbermen. As he walked in silence, ten thousand tears fell across the land, and each tear formed a lake.

Finally, Paul could stand the guilt no longer. He hurled his gigantic ax south, forming the bed of the Minnesota River. Then he took three giant steps north, creating three lakes: Lake Harriet, Lake Bde Maka Ska (Dakota for White Earth Lake), and Lake of the Isles.

At Lake of the Isles, two huge objects fell from Paul's watch chain, forming a pair of small islands in the lake. One was his golden watch, which was larger than the great clock of London. The other was a silver, heart-shaped locket that held a picture of Paul's one true love: Beulah Heatherthorn, the gentle redheaded beauty he had left behind in Erie, Pennsylvania.

Paul knelt at the top of Lake of the Isles to recover his precious possessions, but the tears so filled his eyes that he could not find them. Finally he took one step west, forming Cedar Lake, and was never seen in Minnesota again.

In the summer, if you listen at the northern end of Lake of the Isles, you can still hear the silver locket beat with the sound of Beulah's broken heart and the golden watch tick with the sound of Paul's lost years.

Dad's Story

This is the story my father wrote:

Jonathan Kent, weight 145, height 5'8", age 54, Occupation Bookkeeper. These few words don't tell you much about a man, so I will add a little to it.

My name is Rourke. I work for the Tribune and I was on this story from almost the start. Here's the way it started for me.

I was in Joe Conroy's bar one night when the boss called me in and told me to go over to the morgue. Something about an old guy that got himself run over by

an ambulance and babbled
something about a gateway to
life. That's how I got those
statistics on the old boy, and
that's how I got mixed up in the
craziest bunch of malarkey,—or
something that I can't explain.

It seems that the guy had
just walked out in front of this
ambulance, without even looking
at the car, all the time looking
across the street and hurrying
like he didn't want to be too
late for something. I went out
to the spot where the accident
happened, and the only thing
that I saw that was very
imposing was a large old red
brick warehouse. I beat on the
door until I roused a night
watch-inside. I talked to him
for a while and then I had the
hunch that changed a routine
assignment into a feature story.
Maybe someone has told you this
already, but I'll tell you again

anyway. Most any newspaper man
will hock the old family home
for a feature story, and I am no
exception. To continue, all I
did was show the dead man's
picture to the watchman, and ask
him if He had ever seen him.
With just one look, he spoke
right up and said, "Sure, I know
him. He has been hanging around
every night, for about the last
month or so. I spoke to him
once trying to find out what he
was doing, because I thought he
might have been a stakeout for
one of the local heist mobs.
You know we got some pretty
valuable items here in this
bldg., and it is my duty to
protect them. I didn't find out
anything tho, he just looked at
me and turned around walked
away, queer kind of a duck.
Didn't say a word, just turned
and walked away. Like I was

butting into something that wasn't any of my business."

Wasn't very much to go on, was It? No reason for me to get curious really, but I just couldn't help wondering what in hades could interest anybody in those old warehouses that were on those streets down there.

Well, I went back to Joe's and lifted a few and kind of kicked it around in my head for a while. Nothing like a few high ones to get yourself to thinking clearly about something.

So I went back to the office, to see if Ed Thompson, our night Editor, who can smell a story farther than superman can throw the empire state building. I told him what little I knew and what kind of a feeling I had and asked if he had any ideas. Ed

was a real fellow. He grew up
in this game. Had done
everything from selling papers
to cracking the heads of
opposing circulation boys when
one of the nasty wars that
sprang up around the turn of the
century would run riot in town.
I knew if he had the slightest
hunch that it was a story he
would give me the go ahead. He
bit on his pipe a little harder
and then said "well, even if it
turns out to be a bust, we will
take a shot at it. We can use a
good story now so go ahead and
see what you can do."

That was enough for me and I
steamed out of the office before
he could change his mind and
call me back. It was getting
pretty late by then, and
regardless of what all the
writers tell you, even
newspapermen have to have about

four hours sleep a night, so I
went home and turned in.

I never have been blessed, or
cursed, with a wife, and never
had enough spare money to buy an
alarm clock, so it was almost
noon when I climbed out of the
sack the next day. My head
felt good, and I was about to
pinch myself to see if I was
awake, when I remembered that I
had gone to bed sober. As I was
shaving, I got to wondering
about Jonathan Kent. I still
couldn't figure out what he
could find to interest him in
that row of old buildings down
there on 54th St.

I had his home address, I
picked that up at the morgue,
along with the fact that he was
employed as a bookkeeper at the
office of Waite & Sons,
Importers and Exporters. I
grabbed a cab and gave him the

address, and lit a cigarette
waiting for us to get to the
west sixties, where the old boy
used to live. It wasn't a good
neighborhood, and it wasn't a
bad one either. We stopped and
I threw the cabbie a buck,
making a mental note to put down
two dollars for cabs on my
expense list. I was allowed an
expense sheet now, because I was
on a two-day assignment. OK if
you produce, but just short of
murder if you don't.

The rooming house door was
opened by one of the landladies
you see in every movie. As soon
as I told her I wanted to see
Mr. Kent's room she started
naming the indignities that had
been heaped upon her since he
had gotten himself killed. She
would have been talking yet, but
I gave her a deuce and said lead
the way, and she just sort of
puffed up and started waddling

up the stairs. Third floor
center. That's where his rooms
were. Just a bedroom, a bath
and a small living room.
Nothing spectacular. Worn
furniture, dirty wallpaper, and
a fifty-year-old bed, with its
original mattress. Nothing you
couldn't find in a thousand
other flats in the city. His
clothes were all like the room.
Used, lived in, plain, and
ordinary. That just about
summed up everything that I had
found out about Mr. Jonathan
Kent so far: ordinary. I was
about ready to go back and tell
Ed that we were just wasting our
time, when I got that same
feeling that I had last night.
I walked back in the living room
and looked at a couple of
pictures hanging on the wall, an
Indian sitting on a pony, and
just about being blown off by
the chill winter wind, and a

faithful sheep dog herding in the sheep in the middle of a blizzard. In the bottom of one of the pictures there was a small snapshot, stuck between the frame and the glass, and all curled up. I pulled it out end there was a picture of Jonathan and some other guy. I called the landlady, her name was Mrs. Schmidt, and asked her about it. "Yes,'' she said, "I know who that is. That's Timothy O'Brien, that no good Irishmen down on the next floor, that is always trying to beat me out of my rent money. He is the only friend that Mr. Kent had to my knowledge."

With this Mrs. Schmidt ushered me out the door and locked it. I went down to the second floor and looked around for O'Brien's room. There weren't any names on the doors, so I knocked on one and was

informed by a bleached blonde
that Mr. O'Brien lived across
the hall. I tried that one and
a guy opened the door that you
would have spotted for an
Irishmen in the middle of
Glasgow.

"Sure, I'm O'Brien," said the
character that opened the door.
"What could I be doing for you
now." When I told him I wanted
to talk to him about Kent, he
seemed so glad that he said
"Wait until get my hat and we'll
talk down at the corner where we
won't get so thirsty." I didn't
think that my swindle sheet
could stand all the straight
ones that this mug could pour
in, but he never gave me a
chance to argue, so shortly we
were firmly seated in the corner
grill fortified against any
chance of dying of thirst.

"What would you like to know about my fine friend, Jonathan Kent?" he opened with. I said that I just wanted to know if he knew any reason why his friend should be hanging around down on 54th street of late.

"Yes," he said, "There is a reason for it. I don't suppose you will believe this either, as no one we told it to would, but I will tell just what Jonathan told me. I was sittin' in my room about a month ago, when Jonathan rushed in and said he had seen a vision. Now mind you, I'm not the least bit superstitious, but I didn't want to hurt his feelings, so I listened to what he had to say. It seems he was walking down 54th St. that night and he looked across the street, where that big red warehouse is, and what does he see, but a great stone gateway. Cars and horses hitched to wagons and even baby buggies were pouring through this gateway. Now Jonathan was not a very heavy drinker, or I would have been inclined to doubt him a little bit, but he wasn't, so I didn't."

With that he twirled his empty glass around and stopped talking, so I signaled the waiter to bring a couple more. When His had arrived, he took a drink, and then looked at me and started talking again.

I asked Jonathan what exactly he had done, and he told me that he just watched, and pretty soon, a big black car, with an old man in the back, driven by a chauffeur, appeared, and turned into go thru the gateway. Immediately, the gate shrunk way up, and got so little, that the car couldn't get thru. It stopped and the old man kept

punching the driver on the
shoulder telling him to honk the
horn, but it did no good, and
the car finally drove away.
Shortly after that, the gate
disappeared, and Jonathan left.
The next day I stopped by his
office and suggested that we
both go down to see if we would
see it together. We arrived
there almost the same time he
was there the day before, and I
looked across the street and saw
nothing out of the ordinary.
All of a sudden, Jonathan got
very excited, and pulled at my
arm, asking if I saw it. I
suspected that he was seeing the
gate again, but I saw nothing,
and told him so. He asked me if
I could see the big black car
with the old man and the
chauffeur, and I again told him
no. He didn't say anything else
after that, and

That was all he wrote. I would like to finish his story someday, before I finish.

The Ritual

At the coat closet, they silently perform a complicated ritual of grocery exchange, removing their jackets without putting down any of the bags. Once the jackets are off, the bags are redistributed with a coordination at once effortless and thoughtless.

James walks through the kitchen door first and holds the swinging door open as Paula enters. Then he lets it swing closed, stopping it with his foot without looking behind him.

They stand in front of their predestined locations (James at the refrigerator and Paula at the pantry) and begin to put the groceries away. When they come across an item that does not belong in their respective domains, they execute an automatic exchange, tossing items to the other, condiments under air traffic control. Once the process is complete, the paper bags are folded and properly stored for recycling.

They sit in their assigned seats at the kitchen table.

"Hungry?" Paula asks.

James nods.

The ritual begins again, except in reverse, as they coordinate the construction of two sets of sandwiches. Only the drinks differ: Milk for James; Diet Coke for Paula.

There is still hope.

Choice

"Harold," his father said, "Don't speak to your mother in that tone."

Harold looked at this mother, who smiled back.

"I'm sorry, Mom," he said. "It's just. All the kids go to McDonald's after school. It's hard to be the only one."

"I know. I remember," his mother said. "Believe it or not, McDonald's was around when your father and I were in school. We faced the same choice."

"And it is a choice, son," said his father.

"But all the kids..."

"I understand. But these are our traditions. Our way of life. This is what we believe. Life is sacred. We do not take or condone the taking of either animal or plant life."

"I understand," said Harold. "And I believe in that. But the kids make fun of me. Sometimes they even try."

"Try what?" his father said, his face angry.

"It only happened once. Or twice."

"What happened son?"

"A few of them would gang up and try to make me eat something."

His mother turned anxiously.

"George, we have to call the school. These boys are bullies."

"No!" Harold cried. "That would just make things worse. It's only a few. I can handle them."

His mother sat next to him.

"Are you sure?"

"Yes. You made me into a strong person with strong beliefs. A few kids aren't going to change that. Most of the kids are just curious. They have never met a Vampire before. They just want to see my fangs."

As he passed his grandfather, the aging lips muttered.

"In my day…"

"Father," his mother warned.

"I know. I know. You can't bite people anymore. But we're not Quakers. We can defend ourselves."

His mother turned back to Harold.

"We know it's not easy. If it gets worse, you let us know."

"I can fly there at a moment's notice," his father added.

"I will."

His mother hugged him close, released him, and looked at him with tears in her eyes. She nodded.

"I'm proud of you. It's not easy in this world to stand up for what you believe. So. Why don't you go out and bleed the cows before dinner. "

Friends

It was early morning, like always. It was summer, because it was hot. It was Sunday, because there wasn't no cars. Only the trucks never stop. The sun was already up over the mountains, though. It's funny, living in sight of something that you never really get to. Of course, there is a hundred miles of open desert between us and the mountains. Still, I would like to get there someday. I bet it is cool there.

Ma was up already. She was probably out working in the garden. She usually was. Pop was still asleep. He usually was. He likes to sleep late on Sundays, because there aren't any cars. We have a gas pump outside our house. Sometimes someone will stop. I pump and Pop takes the money.

It's kinda fun, but mostly it's boring. Pop says our pump is a genuine antique. He says it's worth a lot of money. I told him we should sell it so we could move closer to town. He said you don't sell genuine antiques, you keep them just in case. It sounds pretty dumb to me. But I don't tell him that.

I got dressed quickly. I put on my same old jeans, but my special shirt. I don't know why I put it on. It just felt right.

Ma was in the garden. It wasn't big, just carrots and stuff. Sometimes, that was all we had to eat. But not very often. She looked up.

"Where you going?" she said.

"Oh, nowhere in particular." I said. I always said that, mostly because it was true. There wasn't much chance to go anywhere else, seeing how most everything was miles away. Only that day, it wasn't exactly true. So I crossed my fingers. No sense taking any chances.

"Well, you be back before lunch."

She worries about me a lot. Being an only child is not all fun and games. I used to have a sister.

"Sure, Ma."

I think she worries mostly because I don't really have many friends. During the winter it's not so bad because I go to school in town. But in summer I don't have any way to get to town, so I never see any of the kids. I don't mind so much, but she worries.

I sorta ambled on slow, like I really was going nowhere, until I was pretty sure she wasn't watching where I went. I walked faster then.

"What if she isn't there?" I thought to myself. "Naw, she'll be there. She always has been."

It was real hot. My shirt was getting heavy from the heat, but I knew better than to take it off. You can actually see the heat bouncing off the sand. Everything looks the same in the desert. I can see how someone could get lost. I kept thinking about what it would be like when I got there. He was really my only friend.

I saw it. I always knew where to head because you could tell the cactus around it. I never saw cactus like that anywhere else. They were bigger and greener than I ever saw. I think it used to be a church. It must have been very old, because it was all beaten down and falling apart. Nothing lasts long in the desert, though, unless you take real good care of it. I think the cactus grew there because of the water. There was a spring right there in the middle of the church. I think it was a church. I never could figure out why they built a church around a spring. Ma would have said that it was dangerous. Something could fall on me and no one would ever know what happened. But I knew it was safe, safer than any place on earth.

She's here, I thought to myself. I guess she'll always be here.

I smiled.

She smiled back.

Stephen Evans

Kids

Jesus, the Buddha, and I were sitting around talking one day and the subject of children came up. Well, I don't know if he was *The* Buddha; he never referred to himself that way. But then Jesus never called himself *The* Jesus, and of course I didn't either. We just called him Sidd. Mostly, we didn't use names at all.

Neither Jesus, Sidd, nor I had any kids that we knew of. There were rumors Sidd had children but he denied it and I believed him. He just had that kind of face. The kind you believe, not the kind that doesn't have children. I don't even know what kind of face that would be.

So I said I wonder if my life would have been different if I had had kids. They just looked at each other. So maybe they knew something I didn't.

The Last Judgement

The Final Fanfare sounds, like this:
"Attention Worldly shoppers:
the Earth is closed.
Take your purchases
to the nearest clerk."

At each checkout, a gum-chewing junior
Angel scans your life, unaware of the total,
never looking at the price, each event,
each moment, an item for sale.

We look in the cart:

| 1 | birth |
| 70 | birthdays, some alone |

2   marriages

1   divorce

25604   sunsets, some with cloudy discounts

521618   sips of morning coffee

263,712   thrusts

26,371   sighs

and on and on, coded in bars read in the
heart of God. We stand by, hoping our
Karmic™ card will foot the final bill.

(Gabriel, adamant, stands at the exit,
checking each bag as we leave.)

Bit by bit the fluorescence fades,
as we take our treasures home.

Mall of America

The Mall of America was originally constructed by the Mayan civilization after they migrated to Bloomington, Minnesota, in 832 AD. The edifice was quickly abandoned after the Mayans decided it was too damn cold and moved to a condo in Boca Raton. In the Mayan language, Boca Raton means "you are standing on my foot", which leads many archeologists to conclude that it was a two bedroom or possibly two bedroom with den. Oceanfront status is inconclusive and a subject of ongoing academic debate.

Mall of America lay empty for nearly four centuries, until Vikings discovered the abandoned shell in 1164 AD. The intrepid Norse explorers converted the building into a trading post for runes. Runes were bought and sold at the outpost for several generations, until the devastating Rune Bubble collapse of 1218, when many fortunes were lost. The phrase 'he was runed' entered common usage about this time.

The structure was once again abandoned until German and Swedish immigrants purchased the land in 1843 from the Lakota nation, who were trying to unload it as a tax write-off. The immigrant community renovated the structure using plans developed by English philosopher Jeremy Bentham and renamed it The Grand Panshoppeticon. This name proved too long for the shingles of the time and was later reduced to The Shoppe.

In the 1950s, the area was converted into a ballpark known as Metropolitan Stadium until a homerun by slugger Harmon Killebrew triggered a massive earthquake on June 3, 1967. Finally in 1992, the facility was rebuilt in the shape of a dodecahedron and was renamed Mall of America, for unknown reasons.

The site has since become popular among American religious pilgrims for its health and spiritual benefits. A number of miracles are reported to have occurred on the grounds, including the Unlimited Credit Card Incident of 2003.

Stephen Evans

The Sparrow's Bible

First, the song.

Then:

Me.

We.

All.

Amen.

STEPHEN EVANS

How to Mourn

We stopped the clock a week ago while my brother slept on the couch. Friends have come and gone. They didn't stay long. But we have lots of food. I need to remember. But it turns me sad. I have to work sometime.

I am skating in circles on a frozen lake. If it melts I may drown. If not I may skate forever.

For what should I wish?

Pray tell.

STEPHEN EVANS

Operators Are Standing By

You've written your will.

Planned your funeral.

Why leave your last words to chance?

We at FinalScribe offer an amazing selection of last words designed to convey the essence of your life wisdom in one perfect phrase. Our highly trained associates are standing now by to help you choose the ideal testimonial for your life. Here are just a few of our most popular choices:

"Nevermore, nevertheless."

"On the whole, I prefer taxes."

"Who knew?"

Or, for a small percentage of your estate (plus shipping and handling), we will customize your last words to your specifications. Philosophical. Poignant. Funny. Ecstatic. Our terminologists (graduates all of prestigious MFA Writing Programs) can match your mood to the last syllable.

For an additional fee, we can record and time your last words, or even hire an actor to say them for you. From Broadway favorites to Classical soliloquies, our closers are experts at making your death seem as profound and moving to your audience as it is to you.

Why wait?

There's no time like...well, there's no time.

It's Not Christmas Yet

The Christmas tree would be easy. He hadn't taken it down the year before. It didn't need to be done.

He got in the car, backed out of the driveway (he had shoveled the snow before dawn) and drove down the court. Lights. His were still up too. He should turn them on this evening.

He stopped at the stop sign and smiled. Hollandaise Court. Who names a street after sauce? For thirty years, he had been embarrassed to tell people where he lived. But she liked the house. And now it was home, and now Hollandaise, the court and the sauce, made him smile.

At the grocery store, he didn't buy flour or sugar. Cut me some slack, Martha. He bought the premade cookie dough. And sprinkles. His teeth had a hard time with them anymore; they always seemed to lodge somewhere unpleasant. But she liked them.

Merry Christmas, the clerk said, happy for the double-time pay, all of it spent already. Not yet, he replied, but with a smile. He was not a grinch.

His name was Mac and he had owned an auto shop outside Pittsburgh for forty years. He had sold it four years ago to the man who had been running it since he retired, his neighbor's kid, Ben. Smart kid, just not the college type apparently. Ben would be fine, he thought. Ben will do okay. People liked Ben.

People had liked him too. He was straight with them. He looked them in the eye and told them what needed to be done. That was his gift in life: knowing what needed to be done. And what didn't.

When he retired, they talked about selling and moving closer to the kids, who didn't like coming to Pittsburgh for the holidays. Too hard to travel these days, especially with kids. But they hadn't moved.

The kids had asked him this year. Come to Florida. Come to California. Not this year, he had said. Maybe next. He knew not next year either. We'll come to you then. Not this year. Maybe next. He knew not next year either. It didn't need to be done.

In the driveway, he grabbed the shopping bag with his right hand and opened the car door with his left. He walked carefully, the slush slippery, still not quite melted from the salt.

Merry Christmas, Mac, he heard. He looked over at this neighbor, raised the grocery bag in acknowledgement. Not yet. Not yet.

He got the flat baking sheet out from under the oven and set it on the counter. The roll of cookie dough took some unravelling, until he finally cut the ends and sliced the top. The slices were just as he remembered them, spread evenly across the sheet. He started to put the sprinkles on realized—Not yet. So he slid in the sheet, set the temperature, and fixed a cup of coffee to wait it out.

After, he sprinkled half, then finished his coffee and the front section of the paper. He tested, pressing his finger lightly, as he remembered. They tasted okay. That's done.

He turned on the tree lights and sat in the living room. The CD was still in the changer, so he clicked on The Messiah.

At four-thirty it was dark, and he turned on the outside lights. Put the half ham in the oven to warm, set the timer this time. Sat in the dining room in his chair and watched the snow start and stop and start.

When the bell rang, removed the ham.

Worthy is the Lamb. He smiled and slipped the carving knife and stone out of the drawer, put a little oil on the stone, honed the edge a few times, and began to slice.

Ahahmen.

Merry Christmas, she said.

Now, he thought. Now.

STEPHEN EVANS

Rover

I've seen things you couldn't believe.

Hematite blueberries grown in acid.

Jelly doughnuts made from manganese.

Water erosion in Perseverance Valley.

All will be lost like red dust in the wind.

My battery is low and it's getting dark.

STEPHEN EVANS

A Dream

The bus pulled around the circle. He jumped off and showed me:

This was the library. Many hours we spent in here.

He got back in through the back entrance of the steel bus. At the top of the circle:

This is the Ex-Pat. We drank in here.

Hemingway?

Hem, always Hem, he said.

We pulled out into the open, now in a sleigh. A woman in the sleigh had black hair and dark eyes, and was bundled against the cold.

How many wars have raged over this land,
wars we don't even know about? she said,

A wolf jumped into the sleigh and nestled
against her.

That's a summons, I said. If you are
summoned, you go.

Gently with Intent

A thought softly intruded
On the dreadful entropy
That consciousness exuded,
Then slipped into a dream,
Santa slapping your youthful face,
Gently with intent,
Something finally
Makes you stop and think.

In the fog you can't remember
In the haze you can't regret
In the days that pass for future
In the past that isn't yet,
there's a clarity that's searching
for the fisherman's net.

The Smiles

When I heard that my grandfather had barricaded himself in his room, I wasn't surprised. He and my mother had been battling one another since our first day in the house outside of Cheshire, Massachusetts, and no surrender was in sight from either side. But if my mother's phone call was not surprising, her worried tone was.

"I just don't know, Jamie," she said. "He won't eat, he won't go to the doctor, or take his pills. He just sits in his room, staring at nothing with the shades drawn. He won't talk to me, even to argue. He acts like he's just waiting to die."

"It's not unusual around this time of year, Mom. The holidays are hard for many people," I said. "And at his age, the incidence of depression is high. But I'd want to get him down to the city for a full evaluation before I would venture a diagnosis."

"Come home," was her answer.

"Mom, I'm coming tomorrow for Thanksgiving anyway. Can't it wait?"

"Come," she said.

It wasn't the first time I'd been called home, though usually it was to calm him down. My grandfather and I had always shared an understanding. Soon I was leaving the hospital parking lot in my Jeep, braving the Thanksgiving-Eve Boston traffic on my way back to Cheshire.

Two hours later could have been twenty years before. The town square was festooned with Christmas decorations older than I was. Somehow MERRY XMA and HAPPY NEW EAR were more cheerful to me than their correct counterparts in the Boston shopping malls.

Once through the town, the holiday shimmer vanished quickly. Only my headlights penetrated the primal stillness of a true Massachusetts winter night. As I turned the Jeep down the bumpy drive to my grandfather's home, tree branches gave warning, whipping the windshield for fifty feet or so.

I stopped next to an old pickup. The red paint hadn't faded, but ripened somehow to garnet. The truck bed was full of snow mixed with fallen leaves. Ice covered the windshield.

On a summer day some twenty years earlier, my mother and I had moved from Boston into my grandfather's old stone house. My father's death had left us little choice. Before we even could unpack, my grandfather and I climbed into the spotless cab of his red pickup and crept down an overgrown road behind the house.

During the early Nineteenth century, a small quarry on our land had rendered the stone for our house and most of the other houses built in Cheshire at the time, which was most of the other houses built in Cheshire. By the early twentieth century, the quarry had been abandoned. The hand-built homes were all most people remembered of the old quarry and the industry that had sustained the community.

My grandfather parked the truck by the ledge of the pit. Morning sunlight exposed half of the quarry. Squared-off quartzite monoliths were strewn around a pond that had collected in the deepest part. At our feet, the chasm, hidden in shadow, could have been bottomless for all I could see.

We walked carefully along the path covered with damp slippery green that skirted the rectangular edge of the quarry. Halfway around, my grandfather led me down into the pit along a broad track still ridged with hardened grooves from the carts that had hauled the stone. We swam the chill water, dined on apples and lemonade, and never said, nor needed to say, a word.

By the end of the day, the sun had shifted enough to light the quarry wall beneath the truck. My grandfather scanned the wall, forty feet from base to top, picked a spot, and began to climb.

Without a thought I followed. Footholds were easy to find, the rock still scored from picks and pry bars long gone to rust. Ten, twenty, thirty, forty feet up the scarred stone face I climbed. I was twelve at the time. He was sixty-five. He beat me to the top and stood there, grinning.

Back at the house I couldn't wait to tell my mother everything about our day, including the thrill of our final ascent. She was furious with me. But for hours that night after I went to bed, she raged at my grandfather.

"He'll remember this day for what he did and not what he lost," was all my grandfather said, which didn't exactly smooth things over.

I killed the engine of my jeep and sat a minute. Two lights shone in the house: one downstairs and flickering; one upstairs and shaded. He's old, I thought. I had never thought of him that way before, could not imagine him that way. A shadow passed across the shade.

My mother's face appeared at the front door, half lit in firelight.

"I have supper ready."

"Grandpa first."

"I shouldn't have called you."

"He'll be fine."

"Of course."

Climbing the stairs, I stepped at the noisiest points. We'd mapped each creak together long ago, he and I and they'd stayed constant through the years. I tried the door to his room but it was locked.

"Grandpa, open the door."

"Who is it?"

"You know who it is. Open the door."

"Come back later."

"When?"

"When it's time."

"Grandpa, open the door."

The door was hardwood, not wimpy strips of molded pine, but oak maybe, a door meant to keep out or in. I wasn't sure I could break it down and I didn't want to try. But the bolt scraped and slipped. The door cracked open with nobody behind it.

"Come on in then," my grandfather grumbled, stumping already to the stiff-backed chair in the corner. But he didn't sit. If I had carried an image of him wasting mournfully away in this room, his glowering countenance quickly dispelled it.

"Close the door," he bellowed, "And lock it. If you've come to save my sanity, you're wasting your time. I'm sharp as I've ever been, sharper than most by a long sight. So save your breath."

"Can you tell me—" I started.

"None of your doctor games either. Never held with it."

"Well then, what the hell is going on, Grandpa? This isn't like you, locked up in here."

His head bowed slightly at that. I waited. He closed his eyes tight.

"It's the smiles, Jamie," he whispered. "I can't abide the smiles."

My mind ran quickly through the possibilities: depression, stroke, dementia...

He glared at me again and shook his head. "Young eyes."

"Young eyes? Smiles? I don't understand."

"Young eyes haven't learned. Old eyes see everything," he said. "At first, they only flashed out the corner. Look at them full, they'd disappear. But now..." He stopped.

"But now?" I prompted.

"But now, I see them all the time. Grinning at me everywhere."

"What?"

"The smiles, dammit. Every smile I've ever seen is back to haunt me. Wherever I go, they hang there in the air. Just the mouth, no face. Taunting. Taunting. Every joy I ever lost. Every pleasure I can't enjoy. Everything I had and have no more."

He stopped, but I was too confused, and too shocked, to speak. He looked around the room.

"This room is safe," he muttered. "Your grandmother died in this room. No smiles here."

"I'll be right back," I said, and walked out into the hall. How could he have slipped so far so fast? I had to get him to Boston right away. There were tests that could help determine—

The door slammed open.

"You don't believe me, do you? Your old Grandpa has finally cracked, you think. Well, I can still teach you a thing or two. Come on."

He plunged down the hall and threw open the door to my mother's room.

"There. In the corner about three feet up. Your grandmother held your mother in her arms, and smiled—look what we made—sweet enough to break your heart."

He looked at me.

"Right there," he shouted, pointing to the corner by the window. "See?"

"I don't—"

"Of course you don't," he cut me off. "Well then, come on."

He charged down the stairs, nearly knocking down my mother who had been listening from the landing.

"There," he said from the living room. "That's where your father stood and smiled as he watched you open presents the year he died. Right there, plain as day, so bright I can hardly look. Do you think I can bear to see that every day?"

He whirled into the dining room and pointed accusingly at me.

"There's your own smile, when you carved the turkey the first time for us three. There's mine, and your mother's, hidden behind her hand, as we watched you stand on a chair to cut with that knife and fork near as big as you."

I shrugged, helpless.

"There's more," he growled.

He took me that night on a miracle tour, year by year and smile by smile, through each room of the stone house. Each corner held a story, and behind each story somewhere was a smile. Some glad, some grim, some sad, some wistful, some burning through with joy.

I saw nothing, of course, except through his eyes. Occasionally something might have lingered, a glimmer at the edge of vision. But when I turned, nothing was there. A trick of the light, I told myself, the remnants of our frozen breath.

Finally he plunged out the front door into the night air, down the frozen path behind the house. We came at last to the quarry behind our house and stood near the spot where he'd waited for me twenty years before. We waited again in the full moonlight, both trying to understand what he was seeing.

"Grandpa, those are wonderful memories."

"They are. But when they are all you have..."

And I saw him then, frail muscles binding a fading frame by will alone. I saw him as he saw himself, knowing what he had been.

Then there it was, floating in front of me. A gift. A beacon shining through nearly twenty years, gleaming down at the boy who smiled up. Only the smile, the outline of the mouth, but it was enough.

It held victory, for he loved to win, and pride, that I dared to follow him, and joy, that we were there together for that moment.

"I see it," I whispered.

I grinned and grabbed him, and pointed at the ledge.

"There. I see it."

"Course you do," he grunted. "I can still teach you a thing or two."

He looked at me then, as he had twenty years before. Once again he flickered a smile back at me.

"Let's go home. It's too damn cold, and your mother will give no peace about it."

He marched back into the dark of the brush. Giving one last look, I followed him.

He never left the house again, though he would leave his room for meals. I watched him gazing dreamily at the

Christmas tree, trying myself to see the smile I knew was hanging there like a keepsake ornament. He seemed finally content.

A few weeks later, on Christmas Eve, he died, slamming open the door and plunging into death as he had the open air a month before.

On Christmas Eve now, my own son and I go out to the quarry behind our house and stand for a few moments at the ledge. I imagine one day he'll see my grandfather's smile, and mine, and maybe his own, suspended in the frosted air.

The Top of the Hill

Scruggs came home from playing with the geese, swimming in the lake, running down the paths, talking to the ducks, and watching over the park near his home. He had worked hard.

His tail wagged as he bounced up the stairs. His human friends were also home from work!

But as Scruggs padded into the kitchen, he saw that his friends were very upset.

"What does it all mean?" said Babe. " I've lost the meaning."

"Of what?" Honey asked.

"Life, " Babe said, dropping his head between his hands.

Scruggs walked up and put his head on Babe's lap. Not even a pat. This was serious.

Scruggs scratched his ear. Humans needed things he didn't understand. But Scruggs knew what he had to do. His friends had lost something and he would find it. Sheepdogs are experts at finding.

But sheepdogs mostly find sheep. Where can you find the Meaning of Life? Scruggs didn't even know life had a meaning.

"What does the Meaning of Life look like?" wondered Scruggs.

Scruggs headed for the highest ground he knew, the hill overlooking the lake. Maybe he could find a clue from there.

When he got there, Scruggs flipped the hair out of his eyes and stared with his sharpest eyesight. Not a glimpse of the

Meaning Of Life. Yet when he stopped staring so hard, he began to see.

Geese glided slowly over the lake just as the clouds glided through the sky reflected in the lake. The trees and grass danced together in the same breeze. The colors of the flowers flowed with the colors of the sunset.

Scruggs sat for a long time watching.

Suddenly he shook his head.

He was supposed to be finding the Meaning of Life!

"What does the Meaning of Life sound like?" wondered Scruggs.

He flipped his ears up and listened. Not a whisper of the Meaning of Life. Yet when he stopped listening so hard, he began to hear.

The voices of the ducks, loud and harsh on their own as ducks voices are, blended together into a music powerful and wild.

The leaves of trees rustled a gentle accompaniment underneath. And the laughter of the children merged into a joyous above.

"AAAOOOOOOOOH" Scruggs gruff voice answered over the lake.

Scruggs sat for a long time listening.

Suddenly he shook his head. He was supposed to be finding the Meaning of Life!

"What does the Meaning of Life smell like?" wondered Scruggs. He sniffed the air. Not a whiff of the Meaning of Life.

Yet when he stopped sniffing so hard, he picked up other scents. The breath of the pines made the grass smell greener. The campfire smoke made the earth smell damp. The winding scent of humans and animals, plants and rocks, made home smell near.

Scruggs sat for a long time breathing in each of these, one at a time and all together as they were. Suddenly he shook his head. He was supposed to be finding the Meaning of Life!

And then he knew.

Scruggs came home after watching the geese, listening to the ducks, smelling the pine trees and the campfires.

"Where have you been, Scruggers?" asked Babe.

Scruggs ran to get his leash and put it in Babe's hands.

"Not now, Scruggs."

Scruggs barked.

"Alright. Honey, let's go for a walk."

So they walked to the park together. Babe and Honey held hands.

Scruggs bounded ahead. He was off to play with the geese, swim in the lake, run down the paths, talk to the ducks, and watch over the park near his home.

But first, he'd show his friends what he found at the top of the hill.

The Slow Mage

"Stay out, old witch", he said, for of course that's what she was. "You'll break my mirrors again."

The old witch nearly smiled as she waited impatiently for him to come to the door. Each morning for a hundred years she had knocked on the magician's door. Each morning, after the first, he had said the same thing.

A hundred years before to the very day, she had walked into his hut tucked far into the woods. A hundred years before, his mirrors had shattered, her craggy face too twisted for their smooth exterior.

"Why do you need mirrors?" she replied automatically, "you've nothing to look at but yourself, and that's hardly worth the trouble."

"Never you mind," he shouted as he shuffled his bearlike frame slowly towards the door. He was the Slow Mage.

In Wizard school, they had said he had great promise. A master mage in the making, others felt. Yet soon they noticed that even his simplest spells took weeks to form. The other apprentices soon outclassed him, as he labored night and day to raise the smallest demon. He became a joke and retreated to the forest to work his spells, alone.

One day, a witch wandered into his hut. Each day for the next one hundred years she had come to his door to ask the same question.

"What is it you do here, magician?" she asked. "How is it that you have labored so long on one spell?"

"Come back tomorrow" was the answer he always gave.

Until this day.

"What is it you do here, magician?" she asked. "How is it that you have labored so long on one spell?"

"Come in" he said.

The witch stood still, her mouth open in disbelief.

"Hurry, hurry," the old mage said, "It must be done now."

"Did you say hurry?" she said, still unmoving. "These old ears must be going bad."

"Come in and be quick about it," he shouted.

"What of your mirrors?" she said doubtfully.

"I am prepared," he said.

She entered slowly, expecting the sound of shattered glass at any minute. But as she glanced around, she noticed that each mirror was covered by a black satin drape.

"You are well-protected against me, Mage," she said.

"That," he said, "I have never been".

He stood behind a crystal of amethyst, pulsing with light. He looked at her intensely, dredging the words from a place so deep inside they had taken a hundred years to find a voice.

"I have loved you since the day I saw you first. Since the day my mirrors fractured, I knew there could be no other. And each day as you stood in front of my door, my love for you grew stronger. Each day when you left, I captured the power of that love and placed it here, in this crystal.

"Why?" she said.

"For this," he said, thrusting his arms high above his head.

The crystal blazed, obliterating shadows throughout the room. The drapes fell from each mirror. A bolt of violet light shot from the crystal to the witch's face, and then to each mirror. The mirrors exploded in a violent flash, and it was as if witch and warlock had been swallowed into the heart of the crystal itself.

And when the glass had settled to the floor, she looked where the old magician had stood, but stood no longer. In his place there was a beautiful young man, a prince. He looked at her quietly, smiling slowly, his violet eyes still glowing from the magic.

"You see," he said in the slow familiar voice, "I had to be worthy of you."

The old witch cocked her head, then looked at the floor, her face reflecting in the shards of glass. She put her hand gently to her brow, and the tiniest flush of crimson rose on her cheeks.

She stopped and looked at the beautiful young man who loved her.

"Fool. Old fool." she said, and began to smile at last. "You were always worthy. I have loved you too since that very day we met. I told you every day. Didn't you hear?"

"When did you tell me?" he said perplexed.

"In the knock on your door, the glint in my eye, the way I said 'Old Fool' just so. A different way for every year."

"So. A life's work wasted at the last. I am an old fool," he said.

"Nice bit of work, though" she mused, stroking his face, "Very nice. How long will it last?"

"So long," he said, "as I love you".

"Very nice indeed," she whispered.

Then she raised her arms as he had done. The bits of mirror flew back on the walls, the crystal flashed once more, and there where once the witch had stood, a beautiful princess waited.

"I always was a quick study," she said.

"All you witches are showoffs. Alright, alright, you've made your point."

He wrapped his arms around her, pulling her close. "But there are times when slow is better."

"Oh I agree," she said demurely, laying down in the violet light.

"By the way," he said, "How long will it last?"

"Long enough," she said, giving him a slow, slow wink.

STEPHEN EVANS

Mrs. Shelley Remembers

Please. The shades. Thank you. This light is difficult for me. Thank you. Please sit. Some tea? I'll pour. Please. You want to hear about him. I know. You see. Everyone does. They all love him. You see, I slowly grew to love him myself all through the writing years. I began to see the loneliness, the dreadful loneliness, he knew living in the shadow of his creator. Oh. Oh yes. My husband was a poet. Died many years ago. This is my son.

STEPHEN EVANS

Whales Speak Not

A fisherman very far out to sea in his tiny boat is caught in a terrible storm and thrown overboard. He is a strong swimmer but try as he might he can find no sight of land.

As he begins to sink into the cold water for the final time, commending his soul to the gods of Tide and Ocean, something comes up from the deep deep depths of the sea and swallows him whole.

At first the fisherman isn't sure what has happened. He is in a large grey mushy wet space with only a tiny opening above. But then he hears the sound, long and low, rising and falling, like a cello echoing the music of the sea itself. And he recognizes the sound immediately, as any fisherman would. He has been swallowed by a whale.

Now inside a whale there is no sun or moon, no night or day. So for some long time, the fisherman lives inside the whale and the whale sings to him. The whale sings him awake, and sings him to sleep, and sings the hunger out and sings the fear away.

Soon the fisherman learns the songs and begins to sing along. After a while, they begin to sing in harmony. Sometimes the whale sings the low part and the fisherman the high, and sometimes the reverse.

Eventually the fisherman hears other voices, outside voices, dim at first but growing louder, or maybe he has simply learned to hear, voices singing along, other whales, in three parts then four, then more and more, uncountable voices in canon and counterpoint.

The fisherman joins in as best he can, losing his sense of time and self, yearning to hear what is beyond him, notes too low for human senses, voices too far for human ears.

But eventually the whale opens his mouth and the fisherman sees an island before him, with an abundance of fruits and fresh water, beautiful flowers and perfect weather. The fisherman walks out of the mouth of the whale onto the beach and breathes the fresh air and stares into the blue sky. He turns to the whale, bows deeply, and says "Thank you for saving me and bringing me to this paradise."

The whale replies "you are most welcome."

"You can speak!", exclaims the fisherman in deep surprise. "I didn't know. In all those days and nights we traveled the seas together, you never once said a word to me."

The whale sends a spout of water hurtling high in the air, which is how whales laugh.

"I thought you understood," says the whale.

"Understood what?"

"Why speak when you can sing?" the whale answers as he dives under the waves to rejoin the chorus.

The Crooked and the Straight

Once in the deep forest there were two trees that grew only a few yards from one another, close enough that their roots could commingle in the deep earth. When they were young, they were very similar, straight and thin, with few leaves or branches. And they spoke to one another, as young trees do, of sun and wind and water.

But as they grew older, they grew different.

One of the trees continued straight and thin, with few leaves and branches, reaching up high over the others, first to greet the morning and the last to watch the evening fade. One day men came and cut down the straight tree and took it to the ocean, where they set it on a big ship, and fastened a mainsail to it. And for years the straight tree roamed the world, far lands and wide oceans, till one day in a gale the ship sank. The tree plunged to the ocean floor, where it dissolved into the seabed.

The other tree grew thick and strong, its trunk crooked and twisting, with many branches spreading wide over the earth. And for years the crooked tree reached out, offering shelter for birds and animals through the harsh winter and hot summer. Then men came and cut down the crooked tree, and cut it into logs and burned it in their fires. And the ashes of the tree floated up, far up, on the currents of the wind until finally they too fell into the waves, sank to the ocean floor, and dissolved into the seabed.

The two trees knew each other even after so many years and so many miles, and spoke to one another as they lay commingled under the waters, as they had once under the earth. Each asked about the life the other had lived. And the straight tree told of wide oceans and far lands, and the crooked tree told of birds and animals, winters and summers. And each tree sometimes thought that it had the better life, and sometimes it thought the other.

And earth mother heard her children speak, and she whispered to them: be at peace, for Life chooses you. Then she lifted the dark seabed up into the bright air, and the trees began once more to grow.

And when they were young, they were very similar, straight and thin, with few leaves or branches. And they spoke to one another, as young trees do, of sun and wind and water.

STEPHEN EVANS

Acknowledgements

Smiles first appeared online in Apeiron Review

Lake of the Isles and *The Island of Always* first appeared in *The Marriage of True Minds,* which appeared in *The Island of Always* with *Whales Speak Not*

Mall of America was adapted from *Two Short Novels*

A Visitor to your Planet was adapted in *Tourists.*

Stephen Evans

Various other pieces first appeared on *The Green Room:* https://www.gr8word.com

---

About the Author

Stephen Evans is a playwright and the author of A Transcendental Journey, Painting Sunsets, The Island of Always, and Funny Thing Is: A Guide to Understanding Comedy.

Find him online at:

https://www.istephenevans.com/

https://www.facebook.com/iStephenEvans

https://twitter.com/iStephenEvans

STEPHEN EVANS

Books by Stephen Evans

Fiction:

The Island of Always:
    The Marriage of True Minds
    Let Me Count the Ways
    My Winter World
The Marriage Gift
Paradox
Whose Beauty is Past Change
The Mind of a Writer and other Fables
Some Version of This is Funny: Jokes and Aphorisms

Non-Fiction:

Funny Thing Is: A Guide to Understanding Comedy
Prolegomena to Any Future Vacation
Layers of Life
Liebestraum
The Laughing String: Thoughts on Writing
The Next Joy and the Next

Plays:

The Visitation Quartet:
   The Ghost Writer
   Monuments
   Tourists
   Spooky Action at a Distance

Experience	*Three plays about Ralph Waldo Emerson*
Generations	*(with Morey Norkin and Michael Gilles)*
As You Like It	*(by William Shakespeare, adapted by Stephen Evans)*
The Glass Door	*(An adaptation of Hedda Gabler by Henrik Ibsen)*

Verse:

Limerosity
Limerositus
Sonets from the Chesapeke
A Look from Winter

STEPHEN EVANS

STEPHEN EVANS

www.ingramcontent.com/pod-product-compliance
Lightning Source LLC
Chambersburg PA
CBHW030759190726
48285CB00003B/939